STAR WARS

W9-DGO-723

Balance of the Force

Dalmatian Press, LLC, 2005. All rights reserved. Printed in the U.S.A.
The DALMATIAN PRESS name, logo, Big Best Book and Tear and Share are trademarks of Dalmatian Press, LLC,
Franklin, Tennessee 37067. No part of this book may be reproduced or copied in any form without the written
permission from the copyright owner.

Dalmatian
Press

09 10 11 12 CLI 34392 24 23 22 21 20 19
13856 STAR WARS: BALANCE OF THE FORCE

The Death Star

How many TIE Fighters are in this squadron?

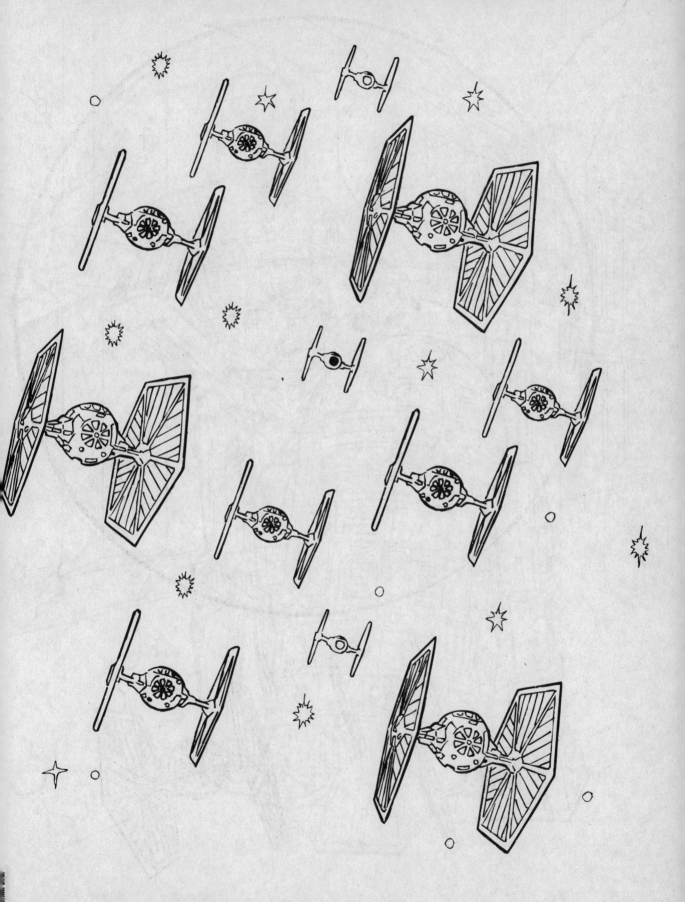

Your answer? _____

R2-D2 and C-3PO on board the *Tantive IV* blockade runner

Darth Vader is strong with the dark side of the Force.

Emperor Palpatine is Darth Vader's master.

The Sith hate the Jedi.

Yoda is a Jedi Master.

Yoda has trained many generations of Jedi.

**Luke has crashed his X-wing
on Dagobah, where Yoda lives.**

**Yoda lifts Luke's X-wing out of the mud,
so Luke can help his friends.**

Yoda trains Luke to be a Jedi.

Training to be a Jedi is hard work.

**Luke goes in a cave and
sees something that frightens him...**

It's Darth Vader!

Darth Vader and Luke Skywalker duel with their lightsabers.

Luke duels valiantly.

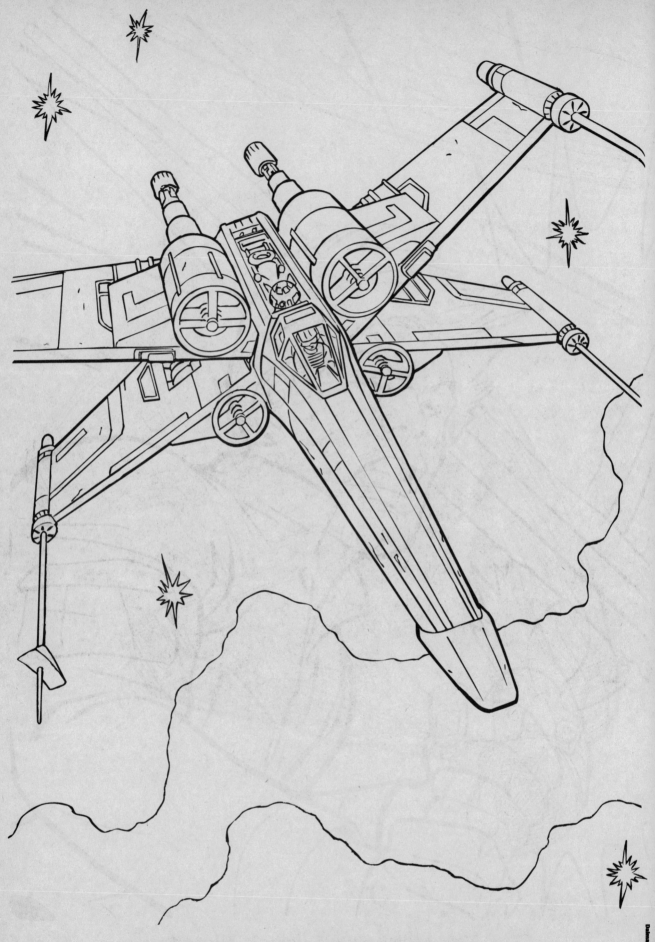

Luke Skywalker flies away in his X-wing fighter.

**The *Millennium Falcon* is piloted
by Han Solo and his Wookiee, Chewbacca.**

Han and Chewbacca blast their way out of trouble.

Darth Vader feels a disturbance in the Force.

© Lucasfilm Ltd.

23

The Rebels have won a great battle.

They reward their heroes with medals.

R2-D2 and C-3P0 have had many adventures.

There are many different kinds of astromech droids. Color the two that are the same.

A

B

C

D

Which two droids are friends? Color them.

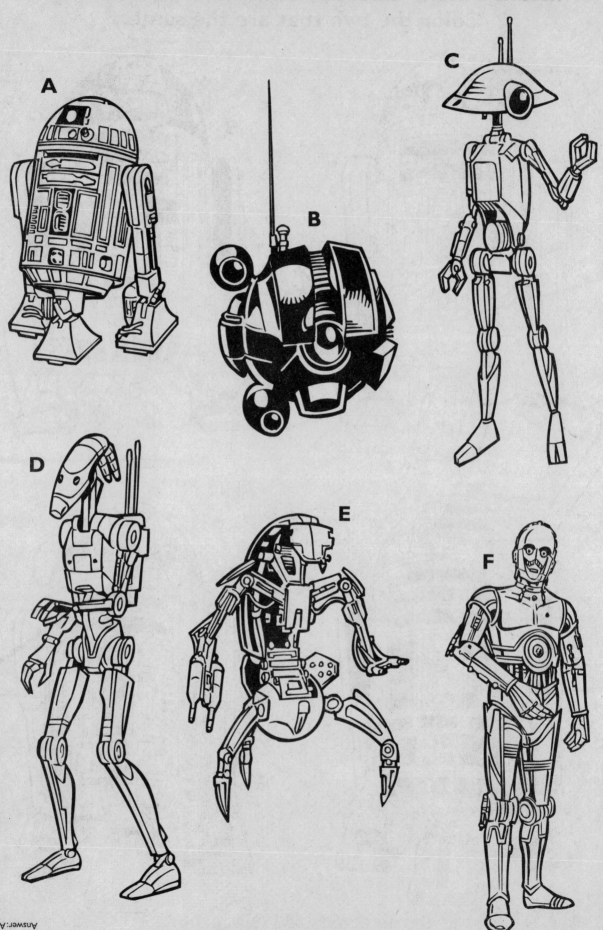

A

B

C

D

E

F

Answer: A and F

2

Some droids are dangerous.

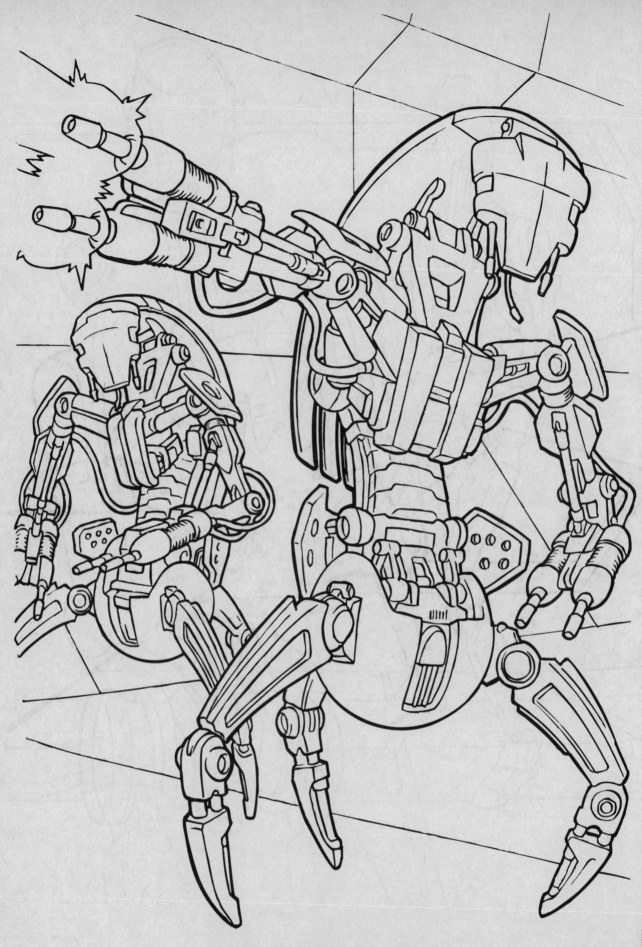

Some droids are big.

Dalmatian Press

Some droids are small.

Which three battle droids are different?

Connect the dots to see what kind of droid helps prepare for the Boonta Eve Podrace.

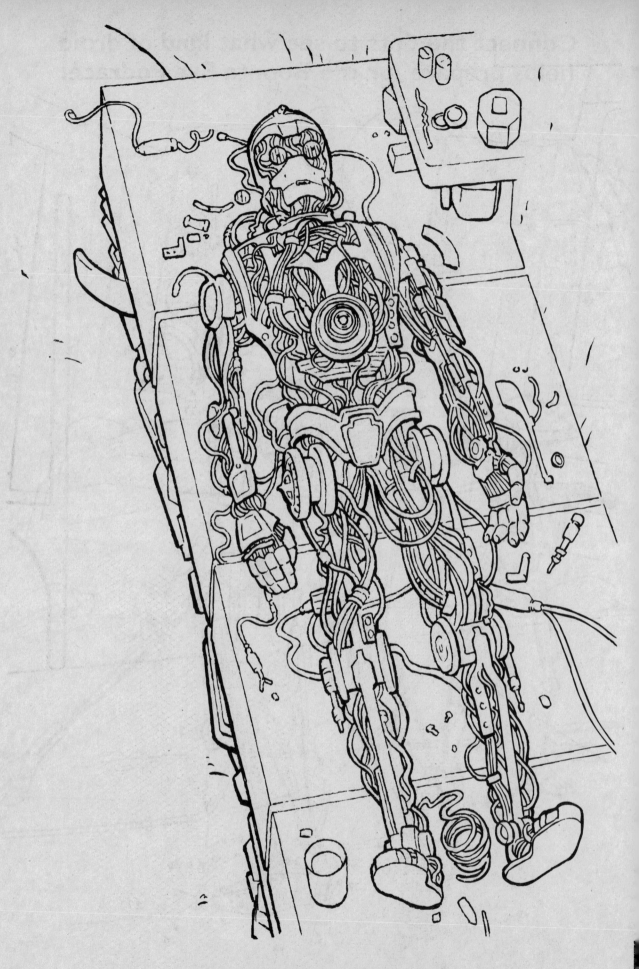

C-3P0 is not quite finished yet.

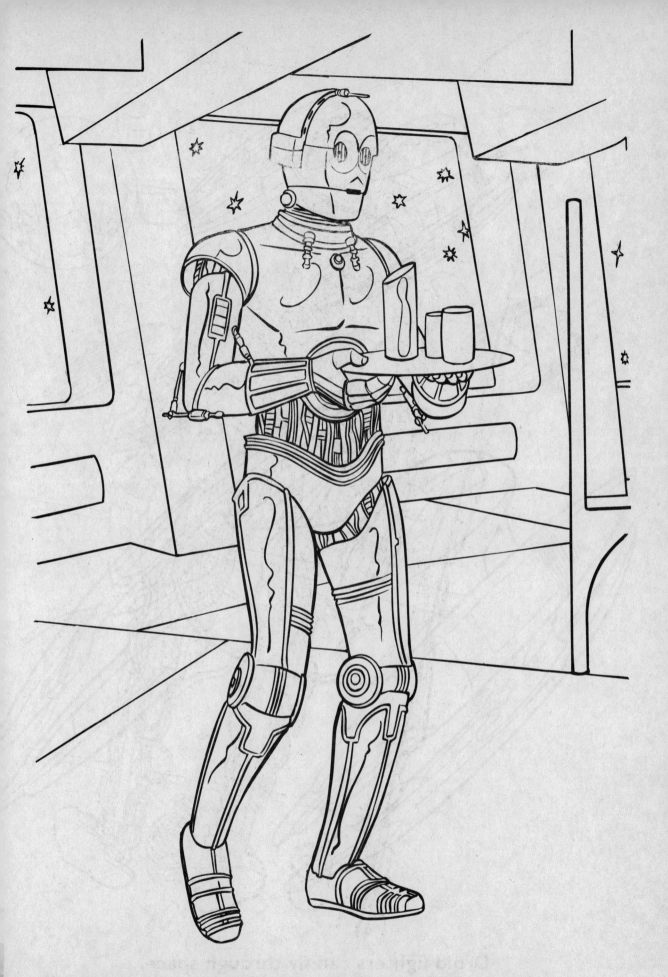

TC-14 brings the waiting Jedi some refreshment.

**Droid fighters can fly through space.
They look like spaceships.**

A Trade Federation battleship

**The Neimoidians from the Trade Federation
are greedy and cowardly.**

Connect the dots to see whom Nute Gunray and Rune Haako are so afraid of.

Darth Maul is a Sith apprentice...

...to his master Darth Sidious, a Sith Lord.

Darth Sidious sends Darth Maul on a mission...

...to capture the escaped Queen Amidala of Naboo.

Queen Amidala of Naboo

Help the Queen land her space cruiser on the planet below.

Qui-Gon Jinn and Anakin run from Darth Maul.

**Darth Maul is a skilled fighter, trained
to use the dark side of the Force.**

Qui-Gon Jinn ignites his lightsaber...

...in a spectacular duel with Darth Maul.

The battle rages on...

Dalmatian Press

**They cross lightsabers as they attack
each other, trying to gain the upper hand.**

The Jedi Council members...

...are the strongest and wisest Jedi in the galaxy.

**High in the stratosphere of Coruscant,
Darth Sidious plans evil ways to destroy the Jedi.**

The Jedi Temple is on Coruscant.

A Jedi starfighter

Anakin Skywalker, Jedi Knight

GRIEVOUS

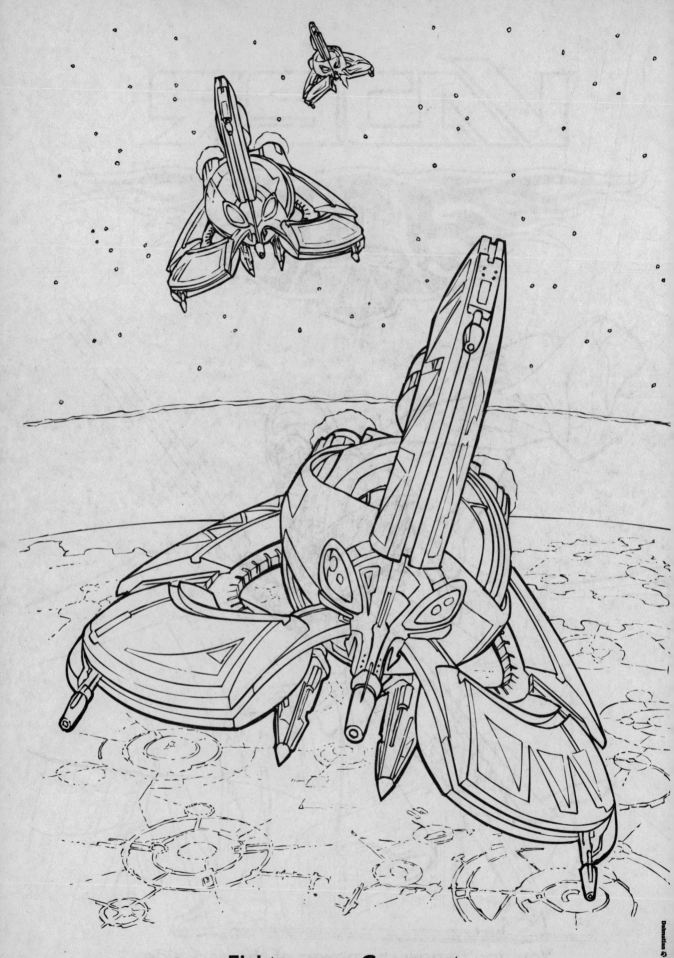

Fighters over Coruscant

You don't know the power of the dark side.

JEDI TRAINING CROSSWORD PUZZLE

Down:

1. Yoda lives on the _____ system.
3. Yoda has long pointy _____ on the sides of his head.

Across:

2. Luke sees _____ in the cave.
4. _____ is a great Jedi Master.
5. On the Dagobah system there are many _____ and other creepy crawly life-forms.

Answers: 1. Dagobah, 2. Darth Vader, 3. ears, 4. Yoda, 5. snakes

Judge me by my size, you will not!

The mighty Wookiee, Chewbacca

Dalmatian ♔ Press

A Jedi starfighter leads a squad of Republic clone fighters

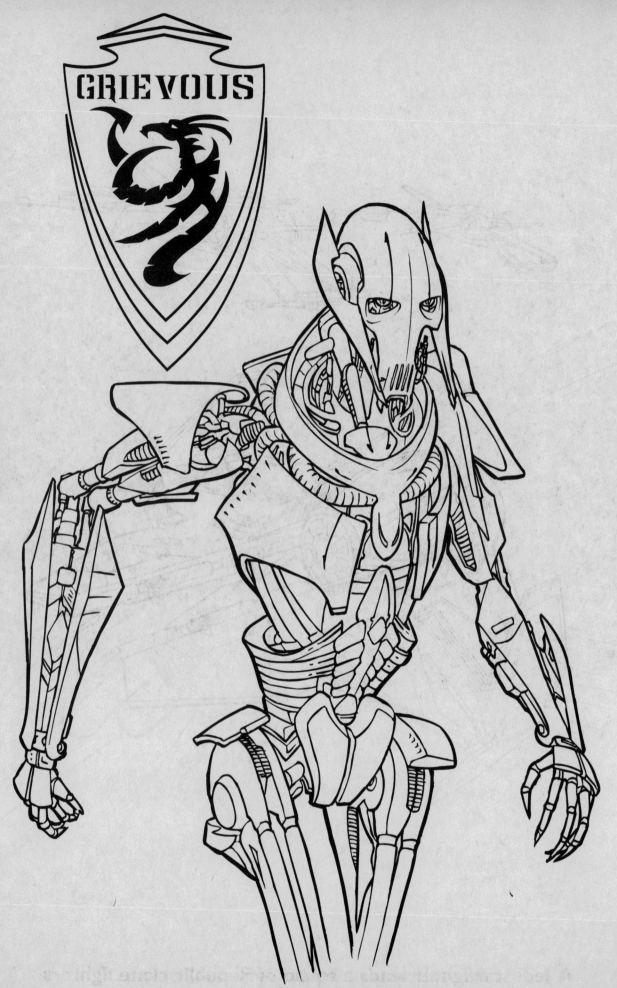

GRIEVOUS

A loyal bodygaurd of General Grievous

A Jedi starfighter is under attack.

Obi-Wan Kenobi, Jedi Master and general in the Clone War

Army of the Republic clone trooper in heavy armor

Dalmatian Press

Clone troopers in battle

DARK SIDE OF THE FORCE CROSSWORD PUZZLE

Down:

1. Last Sith apprentice to Emperor Palpatine.

Across:

2. ____________ Skywalker, father of Luke.
3. The ________ are the sworn enemy of the Jedi.
4. Darth ____________ is the Master of Darth Vader.
5. The color of Darth Vader's lightsaber.

Answers: 1. Darth Vader, 2. Anakin, 3. Sith, 4. Sidious, 5. red

R2-D2 helps navigate Anakin's Jedi starfighter.

Clone troopers attack

Tarfful, a Wookiee soldier

RULE THE UNIVERSE!

Draw yourself as a Sith who uses the dark side of the Force.

JEDI

CLONE TROOPER

GRIEVOUS

DarthVader

VADER'S MAZE

Activate Darth Vader's
life support by making
your way through the
maze on his chest plate.

START

FINISH
ACTIVATE!

Anakin Skywalker attacks...

...the distracted **Mace Windu.**

Mustafar is a volcanic system.

Obi-Wan confronts Darth Vader on Mustafar.

Anakin Skywalker has become Darth Vader.

Chancellor Palpatine reveals himself as Darth Sidious.

General Grievous ignites his lightsaber.

The Separatists arrive on Mustafar.

Obi-Wan and Darth Vader duel with lightsabers.

Clone troopers defend Kashyyyk, homeworld of the Wookiees.

Friends become enemies...

...as Anakin falls to the dark side of the Force.

The Sith have their revenge.

BIG BEST BOOK® to Color

STAR WARS®

Look for more amazing
STAR WARS books to color,
sticker books and activity books
from Dalmatian Press!

U.S.A. $2.99/CAN $4.49

ISBN 1-40371-204-2

9 781403 712042

Spot the Difference!®
P.O. Box 682068
Franklin, TN 37068-2068
Printed in the U.S.A.

THE OFFICIAL STAR WARS WEB SITE
www.starwars.com

13856/0605